One Night with My Neighbor
A.K Wear

Copyright © 2023 by A.K Wear

All rights reserved.

No part of this publication may be reproduced, distributed, or transmitted in any form or by any means, including photocopying, recording, or other electronic or mechanical methods, without the prior written permission of the publisher, except as permitted by U.S. copyright law. For permission requests, contact [include publisher/author contact info].

The story, all names, characters, and incidents portrayed in this production are fictitious. No identification with actual persons (living or deceased), places, buildings, and products is intended or should be inferred.

CONTENTS

Dedication	V
Trigger Warning	VII
PROLOGUE	1
ONE	3
TWO	7
THREE	11
FOUR	15
FIVE	19
SIX	23
SEVEN	27
EIGHT	31
NINE	35
TEN	41
ELEVEN	47
TWELVE	53
THIRTEEN	59
FOURTEEN	65
FIFTEEN	71

SIXTEEN	77
SEVENTEEN	83
EIGHTEEN	89
EPILOGUE: 6 months later	93
More Books	99
About the Author	101

*To the girls that gave and gave and gave
and yet it was never enough.*

TRIGGER WARNING

This book contains themes including but not limited to;
Cheating, fat shaming, body image issues, mentions of parental neglect and abuse, praise, degradation, and drug use.
Your mental health is more important than the story within these pages.

PROLOGUE
Audrey

There is nothing worse than walking in on your long-term boyfriend fucking his assistant on your birthday. But alas, here I am, standing in the doorway of his office. The idiot didn't even bother to lock the door.

I watch, in shock, as he thrusts into her over and over. My voice is stuck in my throat. Even if it wasn't, I don't know if I would have the ability to speak.

His hand is clamping down on her throat as his desk shakes with every hard thrust. He never once did that to me. No matter how many times I asked. No begged.

Minutes go by before either of them acknowledges me. It's only when her head turns to the side and she's facing me that a smile forms on her face.

This bitch is getting fucked by my boyfriend and she has the audacity to smile at me. I can feel my body temperature rise with every thrust he gives her.

Another minute goes by before he turns his head to see what she's staring at.

Our eyes lock and his movements slow. I watch his eyes change from lust to shock. I'm frozen in place, unwilling to move. He pulls out of her, leaving her naked on the edge of the desk, unsatisfied. *I know the feeling, sis.*

He rushes to pull his underwear and pants up, making his way to me.

"Audr–" I don't let him say my name. I won't let him even utter it. Before I even know what I'm doing, my hand goes flying up and across his cheek.

The sting of slapping him in the face rings out in my hand. Without a word, I turn in place and make my way toward the elevator.

"Audrey, honey, wait, please. It wasn't what it looked like."

I won't stop walking. I don't listen to his smug voice. I keep walking, as fast and as far away from me as I can.

I wait for the elevator to open, giving him time to make his way next to me.

"It meant nothing, baby, please." he pleads.

I would believe him. I would even eventually forgive him, if it wasn't the first time I caught him.

This is the first time I've caught him fucking someone else. But over the past ten years, I've seen the hookup apps on his phone. The secret messages he hides from me. Even recently, when he would call and say he was working late.

All the red flags, I ignored them. He had excuses for it all.

As the elevator door opens, I step in, press the lobby button, and watch as the elevator door closes.

But just before it does, I look him dead in the eyes and say, "Fuck. You."

ONE
Audrey

"Bitch! Get up!" My best friend Sami says as she shakes me awake.

I've been in bed for over a week. Sulking. Crying. Eating gallon after gallon of cookie dough ice cream. My hair is going on day four of being unwashed and I haven't changed out of my sweatpants and baggy t-shirt since coming home that day.

The day I found Greg fucking his assistant, I came home, my body radiating with anger. I rushed to change the locks to the apartment. I smashed all of our photos together. And, without shame, I threw his clothes from the fourth floor window onto the street, for everyone walking by to see.

He hasn't stopped calling, texting, and leaving *"I'm sorry,"* voicemails. Each call and text was ignored and every voicemail was deleted.

I crashed from my anger a few hours later and have been in a state of pity since then. Sami came over a few days later after not hearing from me. And so here she is, at my bedside.

"Go away, Sami," I grunt out as I cover myself up with the blanket again.

"Oh no you don't. Get up. We have the fall festival to get ready for. *Remember?!*" She says in her most annoying cheery voice. She uncovers me, pulls me into a sitting position, and drags me toward my bathroom.

I stand in the doorway as I watch her move around in my small bathroom. She starts the shower, takes out a towel from the corner cabinet, and even leaves me to go grab a change of clothes.

It's one thing I love about Sami. She has seen me at my worst and still doesn't judge me for it. She always lets me sulk in my emotions for a few days after any emotional trauma happens. But she's always there to drag me out of it.

I know what she's doing and I love her for it. But the last thing I want to do is go out in public to a stupid fall festival.

Every year, Hollow Creek shuts down the town square and puts on a fall festival. There are carnival rides, food trucks, hay rides, and mazes, and this year they added a fun house attraction.

I always dragged Greg to them. I would always have the time of my life. Riding the Ferris wheel. Paying for overpriced corn dogs. Even getting lost in the corn maze a time or two.

It was all beneath Greg. He was always too good for it. Always complaining about how stupid it is and that it's for kids.

Sami comes back with a set of clothes in her hand. The bathroom is filled with steam from the hot shower, covering the mirror above the sink. It's a good thing because I would hate to see what I look like at this moment.

"Get in and meet me in the living room when you're ready," she says and walks out without another word.

The heat from the shower water feels amazing; relaxing my tense muscles the longer I stay under the spray. I let out a few in the silence. Promising myself, after this, there would be no more tears.

Stepping out of the shower, I wrap myself in a towel and make my way toward the stack of clothes Sami picked out. A simple pair of jeans and a shirt with fall colored leaves painted on it.

Something sparks in me as I look down at this simple outfit laid out for me. It's simple and safe. Like me.

I walk out of the bathroom and make my way toward my closet. What I'm looking for, I don't know.

Thirty minutes later I'm ready.

Wearing a floor length high waisted black skirt and a tan colored loose fitted shirt with the words *"Hallo-queen"* written across it, with a skull and crooked crown. I took the liberty of tying a knot into the shirt giving it a more form fitted look.

I decided on a subtle smokey eye and a deep red lip. Feeling like a new me, I make my way to my closet and grab my black combat boots.

Giving myself one final look in the floor length mirror in the corner of my room, I can't help but feel like a new version of myself. The new me that never got cheated on. A me that didn't give a shit what people thought of her.

With a new determination, I grab my bag off my deck and make my way into the living room. Sami is sitting on the couch, scrolling through her phone.

"Ready," I say standing in the open space.

"Oh bitch! Fuck yes!" The mischievous smile on her face tells me all I need to know. We are going to get into some trouble tonight.

The walk to the town square is short. My apartment building is just a few blocks away. Thankful, yet again, for my choice of shoes.

I know I look amazing. I also feel amazing. As long as I don't think about Greg. Trying desperately to clear my head of what I walked in on a few weeks ago.

Sami wraps her hand with mine as we walk closer to the town square.

"OK, so here's the plan. We are going to ride some rides, eat some overpriced food, and drink like there's no tomorrow." Her voice is mischievous.

Sami is the wild child. The give-no-shits friend. She's taken me on all kinds of crazy adventures throughout the years. All through high school, college, and even now as adults.

Unlike her, I was most comfortable behind a book and under a blanket. I'm the rule follower. I'm the one that stops Sami from going too wild. We are a perfect pair.

She brings a bright spark into my life. And I ground her from flying into outer space.

The best of friends.

But maybe tonight we both can let loose.

TWO
Hayden

The smoke in my room is reflected off of the multicolored lights lining my ceiling. The music pumps through my speakers as I let the high settle in my lungs.

"When did you want to head out?" my best friend Marcus asks.

He's dragging me to the town square for the stupid fall festival. He says it might be good to get our faces out there since the tattoo shop will be opening soon, hopefully.

Every year this stupid small town in the bum fuck of Texas shuts the town square down and fills the streets with carnival rides, corn mazes, and trick-or-treating for the kids. They advertised a scary walk-through fun house this year.

It is the only reason I am going.

"Let's go," I say sitting up at the edge of my bed, "the sooner we go the sooner we can leave." The last thing I want to be doing is being around the people of this town.

In the few weeks we've lived here, everyone has made it known Marcus and I are not welcome. No matter how nice I am. Or how big I smile at everyone. They made up their minds about us the second they looked at us.

My eyebrow piercing. My tattoos cover both my arms, chest, and up my neck. It's all a deterrent for them. They judge me and think they know me even before ever saying a word.

I've always been an outcast. The one everyone avoids. My circle of friends is small. Marcus is only one of five people I have ever let into my life.

I turn the lights and music off before packing a few more joints in my leather jacket pocket as Marcus and I leave my room.

Locking my apartment door behind us as we make our way outside and onto the busy street. Everyone is walking in one direction. Like a herd of sheep.

The speakers atop the light poles fill the autumn air with Thriller by Micheal Jackson.

The closer we get, the louder the screams and laughter become. We walk right up to the large Ferris wheel. Flashing rainbow lights go round and round with each bucket.

Food trucks line the streets around the square. To the left are some carnival games. And to the right a corn maze.

More laughter and screams fill my ears and I can't help but cringe. I want nothing more than to go home. Lose myself in my music, my art, and my weed. But Marcus seems to always drag me out into the world.

He's been my best friend even before I can remember. His parents and mine were best of friends and he and I went to every school together. Up until his dad divorced his mom and left them with nothing. That's when she moved back home to her parents and Marcus stayed with me and my family.

Us being just juniors in high school at the time, Marcus begged his mom for him to stay and finish high school and I begged mine for him to move into one of the million spare rooms we had.

My parents are nepo babies. Both of them. Each coming from family fortunes they didn't make themselves.

My grandparents on my mother's side hit it big in the stock market. My father's parents own a chain of outdoor living stores throughout the South.

Money was the center of my family. The more they had the more they ignored me. And throughout high school, it's the way I wanted it. They only said yes to Marcus moving in because they knew it would shut me up and they could go back to ignoring me.

I was the baby they didn't see coming or even want. I was raised by nannies. But my mother would get jealous of every one of them once I got too attached. It's as if she could sense it.

I learned very quickly to hide my emotions toward them or anything in general.

My black combat boots hit the street as Marcus and I walk up to the line to buy our entry tickets. More laughter and screams.

Mindless couples and parents talking about the first ride they want to visit or the food they want to eat. As if this festival doesn't last all weekend and they won't be back tomorrow night. They don't dare miss a thing.

The line moves slowly, it's a good thirty minutes before Marcus and I make it to the ticket stand. A large orange and black banner hangs from the top reading, "tickets."

The old lady on the other hand asks us how many tickets we need with wide eyes. It's the same look everyone gives us. As if they are looking at the Devil himself. We've gotten used to it at this point.

"Two ma'am," Marcus says with his best fake smile. He hands her a twenty-dollar bill and takes the wristbands from her.

We walk past the ticket stand and right into a swarm of people, walking in every direction. A woman runs my foot over with the double baby stroller. She looks at me as if I was in her way.

Fucking bitch.

"You wanna grab a bite before we head to the funhouse?" Marcus asks, pointing to the line of food trucks. Everything from nachos to full turkey legs.

It's then that I see her. Everything else fades away. Her bright smile framed her full red lips. Her wide hips as she stands next to a group of people. A full head of pitch black hair falls past her plump breasts in loose curls.

I can't help but think to myself, this night just got a whole lot more interesting.

THREE
Audrey

"Don't look but there's a guy to your left and he is staring at you," Sami says as she takes a bite of her salted pretzel.

We've been here for just about an hour. The first thing we did was grab a bite to eat. We ended up running into some friends and have been sitting here at some picnic tables, eating and chatting.

"Who?" I ask as I turn my head and look past the crowds of people.

Even from this distance, I can feel the heat radiating off of him. His deep gray eyes pierce me. His tall thin figure stands above most people that walk past. His dark hair is slicked back.

A silver metal ring sits in the corner of his eyebrow and his arms are covered in artwork. But it's the firefly around his throat that catches my attention.

I know what I must look like, ogling at a complete stranger as my eyes take in his body. Black combat boots, very similar to mine, skin tight black jeans with a few holes showing off his firm muscular legs. A leather jacket covers the loose shirt.

Everything about him, I should look away from. Everything about him should have me running in the other direction. But yet here I am, frozen in place, unmoving. It's not fear I feel as we stare at each other.

It's something else. Something warmer. Wetter.

"Who is that?" I ask, breaking a staring contest and bringing my attention back to Sami and our group.

"Have no clue but it seems like you're about to find out." She smiles at me as her eyes go wide. "He's walking over here, right now."

Panic starts to settle in the pit of my stomach, and I start to flatten down my shirt and skirt. Setting my half eaten pretzel on the table, my body tenses as I feel the air stiffen around me. His shadow even in the glow of the sunset covers me.

"Excuse me," the deep voice vibrating my entire body says. I have to crane my neck to look at him fully as he stands a foot taller than me.

My voice is stuck in my throat as my brain misfires trying to come up with something to say to him. Anything. Nothing comes to me as he stares into my eyes. I feel exposed as if he could see into my soul. The longer he and I stare at each other, the more I get lost in those smokey eyes of his.

"How can we help you gentlemen," Sami comes up beside me, hooking her arm with mine, saving me from embarrassing myself any longer.

"We were wondering if you ladies would like to join us on some rides?" The other voice next to this stranger says. But he and I haven't broken eye contact. Those gray eyes are sucking me, fading everything else around away.

What is this feeling?

ONE NIGHT WITH MY NEIGHBOR

"We were just about to walk a lap around to see everything that there is. Would y'all like to join us?" Sami says and my heart rate begins to pick up even more.

"Y'all can join us," I finally say as I take in a breath of the cool air.

Oh my GOD! What has come over me? I don't know this man, I shouldn't be inviting him anywhere.

He must like that idea though, evident in the slow lift of the corners of his lips.

Standing this close to this man has every part of my body vibrating with a feeling I'm not familiar with. It's as if I've been shocked and the electricity is coursing through my body.

In the ten years I was with Greg, I have never felt this type of feeling.

This feeling is new. And it feels dangerous.

The old me would have ran in the opposite direction from this man. But this new me has me salivating at the thought of spending the night with him.

What his hands would feel like. Or his lips. Or even his cock.

That thought alone has me forcing a mouth full of saliva down my throat.

His eyes land on my throat and he shamelessly licks his lips.

Fuck. I'm in trouble.

Sami breaks me from the spell this man has been under and turns me to face her. "Gentlemen, give us just a sec, would ya." She doesn't wait for their reply as she drags me away. My eyes look back at the stranger.

Mystery man's eyes never leave mine until Sami and I are out of view behind a yellow food truck.

"Ohmygod bitch, he was totally eye fucking you," she says with her gleeful laugh.

"He was not," I retort, knowing damn well I'm lying. He totally was and I was right back.

"OK, here's the plan, I'll go with his friend and our group around one part of the square, and you go with the mystery man to the other side. And we'll meet somewhere in the middle, *eventually.*" her eyebrows rise and fall at the word eventually.

"I don't even know him," I argue. "What if.."

"What if you have the time of your life and forget your stupid lying cheating asshole of an ex-boyfriend that, let's face it, you wasted ten years on."

Ouch. The truth really does hurt sometimes. But deep down I know she's right. I know everything I did for Greg was a complete waste of my time. He never appreciated me or put much effort into us as a couple.

"Ok, but I'm not sleeping with him." I want to so desperately but I don't know this man. I don't know who he is or where he's from. But maybe that's the appeal of him.

I *don't* know him. I probably won't ever see him after tonight.

The old me would have fought this. Would have been too embarrassed to say yes. But this new me, the me I plan on being from now on, has me smiling and agreeing to her plan.

"OK, but if I end up on the 5 o'clock news tomorrow... I will haunt you," I try to sound serious but I can't help laughing at my threat.

"Deal," she laughs and hugs me.

We make our way back to the two guys waiting for us. The stranger doesn't notice me at first but when we get closer his friend nudges him. His eyes land on me and the heat from before returns with a vengeance.

FOUR
Hayden

I try my damndest to hide my growing erection but it's no use.

The way her hips sway from side to side. Her hair getting caught in the cool breeze. Everything about this woman has me vibrating with need.

As she and her friend come walking back toward us, I don't miss the redness in her cheeks. Something tells me they are planning something and I might be a fan of whatever it is.

"Alright boys," her friend says as they stand toe to toe with Marcus and me. "You big fella are gonna go with Audrey and walk one side of the fair," she points at me with an all knowing smile. I can't help but smile back in agreement.

Her name is Audrey. I lock eyes with her. Knowing her name seems a bit too personal but I have this need to know more than just her name.

I want to know what she looks like on her knees. What she looks like taking my cock. What she must sound like when she moans in ecstasy. I plan to find out as much as I can tonight.

"Yes ma'am," I laughed out, never breaking eye contact with Audrey. Her friend says something else but I've completely stopped listening. Nothing else seems to matter at this moment.

"Ready my little black cat?" I look down at her, waiting for her to react. At the sound of my voice her eyes darken and she seems to stand up a few inches taller, still well under my height.

"We'll go this way," I say pointing toward the corn maze. "How's that sound, Audrey?"

Without a word, she takes in a breath and nods her head in agreement. I watch as she turns to her friend and hugs her. Her friend whispers something in her ear and looks at me with a *take care of my friend*, look in her eyes.

And I plan on doing just that.

I give Marcus a look that tells him to behave and he winks at me. He probably has the same idea that I do. Tonight, we both will be having more fun than we first imagined when we got here.

As we part ways with Marcus and her friend, I lead Audrey through the crowd of people. I lace my fingers together so I don't lose her as we walk side by side toward the corn maze.

Her touch is warm in my hand. I can feel her racing heartbeat at the apex of her wrist. It picks up pace as we walk closer to the corn maze.

"So tell me about yourself, Audrey," starting small talk to get her mind off of the fact that her friend just left her alone with a complete stranger.

A stranger who plans on having her in every way imaginable tonight.

She looks up at me confused. Her eyes are full of wonder trying to come up with an answer to the simplest question.

A few more silent steps through the crowd she finally breaks her silence and begins to talk.

"Well, I'm Audrey. I'm twenty-eight years old. I've lived in Hollow Creek my whole life. I got my degree in business marketing and up until very recently I had a long term boyfriend."

The mention of another man has my grip on her hand tightening slightly. Not enough to hurt her but enough to say I have no intentions of mentioning him again.

But being the sadist that I am, I ask, "what happened?"

Without missing a beat she says, "I found him fucking his assistant in his office on my birthday." Her tone is full of emotion. It's laced with anger and sadness at the same time.

"His loss. He's a fucking idiot to cheat on you," I say flatly.

She stops mid-step, turns her head, and looks up at me. I can tell she's fighting back tears at the moment.

"Thanks," she says. "Sami dragged me out tonight trying to help me forget about him. At least that's the plan. And I'm doing a bad job at it." Her nervous laugh hits my ears, filling my heart with a need to help her do just that.

We make it to the entrance of the corn maze and we wait in the short line. Like myself, she has a wristband allowing her to go on any rides or attractions throughout the night.

"How can I help?" I ask, wanting a very specific answer from her.

She looks up at me confused at my question as we step closer to the start of the corn maze. The worker at the start of the maze lets the couple in front of us enter while Audrey and I wait.

She doesn't answer at first. Not until we are let through the entrance of the maze. I take her hand into mine once again and we make a few turns until we end up at a dead end.

"What's your name?" she asks, completely avoiding my question from earlier.

"Hayden," I answer as I lead her to another turn in the corn maze. We walk hand in hand down a long path and make a left turn. It leads us into what feels like a circle and into another dead end.

"Hayden," she whispers. My name on her lips hardens my already throbbing dick. I turn to face her. Nervousness is written all over her, she's looking everywhere but at me.

"Yes," I answered, looking down at her. I test my luck as I fill a free strand of her hair behind her ear.

"I know how you can help me forget," she says leaning into my hand. Her cheek feels warm. I keep her in my hold, not wanting this moment or any moment with her to end.

"How's that my little black cat," I whisper. I know what's coming. I know what she needs, what she wants at this moment. But I need her to say it.

She tilts her head up at me. Her hazel eyes are full of need and want. But I can sense she's fighting whatever she's trying to ask of me.

If I have to wait till the sun rises for her to answer, I will. There is nowhere else I'd rather be in this moment than right here with her.

"Kiss me," she finally breathes out.

FIVE
Audrey

"Kiss me," I say. Not wanting anything else at this moment.

He doesn't let a second go by before his lips crash into mine. Warmth invades me as I give him full access to my mouth. His touch plays with mine and in that moment I feel the coolness of metal hit my senses.

A tongue ring. He has a tongue ring. The contract of the cold metal bar and the warmth of his mouth has my body melting into his hold.

A part of me wants to pull away. I want to apologize and walk away. Forget everything about this moment. But another part, a bigger part, never wants this moment to end.

The old me always hoped a man would grab me and take complete control. Greg never once did that. I was always the one instigating our sex. We never shared a kiss quite like the one I'm sharing with Hayden.

As we continue to fight for control with our tongues, a second goes by and I give in. Letting him invade every inch of me. He starts to move our connected bodies until my back hits a wooden board. The boards make sure that no one ventures into the corn and stays on the given paths.

I feel his hand run up my arm, his fingers leaving a trail of goosebumps. When he reaches my shoulder his touch goes soft as his fingers run along my collarbone. A small shiver runs along my spine at the feel.

When he gets to my throat, he stops. He breaks our kiss but keeps our foreheads connected. Both of us are breathless. Air can't fill my lungs fast enough and my heart is pounding in my chest.

"I could get addicted to the taste of you black cat," he grunts out as if pulling away from our kiss hurts him as much as it hurts me.

His darkened eyes are full of the same emotion mine are.
Want. Need.

"Don't stop," I all but beg. This new me knows what she wants and will make sure she gets it. And she knows Hayden will be the one to give them all to me, if not just for tonight. "Please," I let out.

"You are beautiful when you beg," he whispers as he runs his wet lips down from behind my ear and across my sensitive throat.

"Please, Hayden. Please kiss me again." I plead with him. Wanting, needing him to give me this one thing.

"I have a better idea my black cat." the devilish smirk on his face reaches mine. Whatever his idea, I know I won't fight him. I'll take whatever he's willing to give me.

He steps back from me, leaving a foot of space between us. It's too much. I can see him trying to find the words.

"Let me ask you a question," he runs his eyes up and down my body. Even though I am fully clothed, minus the small strip of skin across my belly where the t-shirt knot has ridden up my stomach.

His eyes stay there staring at the small piece of exposed skin. He licks his lips and snaps and focuses back on my eyes.

"Have you ever done anything like this before?" His question takes me back. It's a bit personal. But he has every right to ask because we don't know each other.

I shake my head vigorously, not breaking eye contact. My relationships have been safe. Never adventurous.

"You've been a good girl your whole life. How about tonight, you be my bad girl."

His comment about me being a good girl my whole life hits the nail right on the head. If Hayden, a stranger, can read me so well, what does that say about the people who really know me?

It's true though. I got good grades. Never stayed out past curfew. Prom night was spent dancing and having a good night. It ended with Greg dropping me off at my front door. My parents sent me to the state college. I studied hard. Graduated Summa Cum Laude and got hired at Hartman Management three months later.

I behaved and did as I was supposed to do my whole life. I haven't had time for true excitement in my life. No moment where I just said *"fuck it"* and lived for the consequences.

This is that moment. I can feel it. I know it. So I do the one thing the old me would only wish she would do.

"Yes," I say confidently, without a single thought running through me except this moment right now.

I watch him invade my space again. He towers over me as he grabs my chin, lifts it, and says, "good girl,"

He slams his lips onto mine once again. I can't help but let out a moan at the feel of him. His hands start to roam all over my body. I feel him everywhere.

He glides his hand over my throat as he breaks our kiss once again. He lets out a laugh as I groan in frustration. His grip on my throat tightens slightly.

The air in my lungs gets stuck. I should be scared. I should tell him to stop. But something in me wants more. Wants whatever he is willing to give me.

An evil smile forms on his lips and his eyes turn a deep shade of midnight. "My black cat wants to play, is that right?"

I nod, unable to speak. But he releases the pressure around my neck before saying, "your words are very important in this situation my little black cat."

He doesn't move, waiting for my response, "yes," I let out a rough reply. "I want to play,"

"That's my good girl. Now I'm going to put my hand back around your throat while I have my fun with you."

My eyes go wide with his bluntness. No one has ever spoken to me or about me in that way. Greg was one of those silent lovers if you could even call him a lover.

"Yes please," I moan, unable to hold back my desire for this man any longer.

SIX
Hayden

I can feel her pulse as I wrap my hand around her neck again. The sweet smell of citrus invades my senses as I run my nose along her chin.

I fall to my knees ready to worship this woman in this corn maze. The faint noises of people walking by through the maze surround us.

With one hand still around her neck I run my free hand under her skirt. My fingers glide up her smooth legs until I feel the soft fabric of lace at her hip.

"Tell me black cat, are you already wet for me? Does the idea of me eating you out in this corn maze turn you on?" I look up at her.

"Yes," she moans as I run my fingers along the edges of her panties.

Her body tenses when I run the pad of my hand over the top of the fabric at her pussy.

"Oh god, yes please," even in the shadows of the corn maze, I can see the redness in her cheeks. She's lost in this moment, just how I want her. She's letting herself feel everything.

"You sound so pretty when you beg. Should I make you beg some more?" I add more pressure to her entrance with my hand.

Without waiting for her response I pull away as I feel her body start to tense with her orgasm on the horizon.

"No. no no no," she whines and I can't help but laugh. She is so needy. So full of lust. Whoever left this woman is an idiot.

I slowly stand back onto my feet, leaving my hand cupped at her pussy. Her skirt has ridden up, exposing her legs and pussy.

"My little black cat, I'm going to have so much fun with you." I kiss her once more as I hold her neck in place with my hand. I can't get enough of her.

Her lips, her warm skin, the feel of her invading all my senses. She is going to be such a fun toy to play with tonight.

Putting her and myself out of our misery, I slip my hand past her panties and open her soaked pussy lips.

Her moan is muffled as my lips slam into her. This time I don't let go or stop.

I slide one, two, and three fingers inside of her. She's on her tiptoes as she tries to stand up straight from the pleasure I'm giving her.

Her hands hang on top of my shoulders and she stretches her fingers into my hair. Her touch is soft, her long nails running along my scalp.

The feeling sends a shiver down my spine.

Our lips clash together. She tastes of mint and citrus. An addicting scent. I want to bottle it up and jack off to it any chance I get.

"Hayden, please," she moans through her lips. She's wrapped her legs around me now. We are pressed against the wood beams and corn stocks.

My fingers continue to slide in and out of her. The sound and feel of her wetness has my dick hardening painfully in my pants.

Our bodies are grinding in rhythm, reaching closer and closer to her orgasm. I reach behind her neck to support her head as I finger her.

"That feels, oh my god. That feels..." Her train of thought is derailed when we hear a group of people on the other side of the wall of cornstock.

Her eyes go wide with shock and embarrassment. I can see her starting to tense, but I don't stop, wanting and needing her to come.

"Oh my little black cat, don't get quiet on me. Let me hear that sweet voice when you come on my hand." I work my fingers faster into her, reaching that special little spot inside of her.

Her head falls onto my shoulder as she screams out her ecstasy. Her legs shake around my hips. I'm holding all her body weight now in her aftershock. Her body goes limp post orgasm.

I keep holding her as I remove my soaked fingers from her pussy. Bringing my fingers to my mouth, I can't help but taste the sweetness of her.

She lifts her head off my shoulders just in time to see me suck on my fingers. Her eyes are glazed over post orgasm.

She removes her wrapped legs off my hips and she finds her balance back on the ground. Fixing her skirt and shirt back into place, her eyes don't leave mine

"I've never," her face goes emotionless. Her eyes fall to the ground at the realization of her train of thought.

"Never..." I say lifting her chin with my pointer finger, "never had an orgasm. Never been fingered." I laugh but her face is now full of shame.

"I've never orgasmed. Or at least not like that." she finally says since she has nowhere to look but up at me.

"Well my little black cat, I'm glad I could be the one. Now what do you say we finish this corn maze and go get something to eat."

Stepping away from her, I hold out my hand for her to take. She looks at it suspiciously but takes it regardless.

"Whoever he was, is an idiot," I whisper into her ear, leaning her into me. I lead her through the maze until we see the large arch signaling we've reached the end.

Walking out of the maze, I lead us toward the food trucks. "What are you hungry for?" I ask, trying to not lace my comment with any sexual tension.

We stand back far enough for her to see more than one food truck at once as her head whips back and forth trying to take them all in.

I love the feel of her hand in mine as we just stand here. Crowds of people are walking around us but I can only see and feel her near me. I can't help but run my thumb across her knuckles.

SEVEN
Audrey

The warmth of his touch in my hand feels so good. It's a simple act but if only he knew what it meant to me.

Greg never wanted to hold hands or show any affection in public. He would always say that it wasn't appropriate. Apparently, it is appropriate to fuck your assistant on your desk but who am I to say.

"I think I'll just do the cheese nachos," I say, not telling him what I want is to add more than that. But again the words of Greg come flooding back.

"How about you get a salad?"
"Why don't you ask for a diet soda, or just do water,"
"We can always split the plate that way you don't eat too much,"

Guilt and shame fill me. I know I'm not the thinnest person. But I love my body. I have curves and I love that about myself. No matter how often Greg asked me to slim down, in so many words.

"What else?" Hayden looks down at me. I really hope he can't see me and my shame. "What other toppings do you want black cat?"

His nickname for me is silly but it warms me throughout my body. I don't know why I keep comparing him to Greg but in the past hour we've been together, he has been everything Greg hasn't been in the past ten years.

Hayden has been kind, sweet, and oh-so-giving, and the memory of the corn maze comes flooding back.

The way his fingers felt inside me. The way his hand felt around my throat. His warm lips as he kissed me. Greg never did any of those things, no matter how many times I begged to be more adventurous in and out of the bedroom.

We've moved up to the window to place our order and I wait for Hayden to start. He gives his order for a loaded hot dog and a large fountain drink in one of those souvenir cups.

When he finishes he looks down at me, "your turn black cat."

I want so desperately to load my nachos with everything but the old me starts to creep back in. The old me tells me he wouldn't like me stuffing my face. It wouldn't be ladylike.

Pretending to look over their posted menu again, I push the old me back down and say *fuck it.*

"I'd like your loaded nachos," I pause and look up at Hayden. His smile edges me on. "With beef, nacho cheese, onion, tomato, beans, and sour cream." I feel breathless as I tell the woman over the window my order. "With a large lemonade," I add. "Please."

"Atta girl," Hayden smirks and nudges me with his shoulder. I can't help but smile up at him. His simple praise covers my body in warmth.

The woman smiles down at me and starts to tap on her tablet. She gives us the total and I go to pull out my cash from the pocket of my skirt.

Hayden stops me as he pulls his wallet out faster and hands her his card. She taps it on the small card reader and hands it back to him. I would argue but his raised eyebrow tells me I shouldn't.

We step to the next window and wait for our food to be made.

Thirty minutes go by as Hayden and I sit at a picnic table across the street and eat our food. The loaded nachos do their job and fill me up.

Even though I don't know much about Hayden, the conversation flows great. Not much silence other than when we both have food in our mouths.

He told me that he just moved into town with his best friend. I tell him that I grew up in this town.

He tells me he's opening up a tattoo shop somewhere in town and I tell him that I have dreams of opening up my own bookstore.

It's easy to open up to him, to tell him my wants and dreams.

It's at the moment that I have the last bite of my loaded nachos and I'm people watching that I see an all too familiar face.

Greg.

My heart starts to race and I feel a soft touch on my shoulder.

"You ok?" Hayden asks and I shake myself out of the haze Greg has me in. But just as I'm about to look away, I see it.

He's holding hands with her. Abby. His assistant. The woman I saw him fucking on his desk that morning. The memory comes flooding back.

I can feel my heart rate rise, my palms become sweaty, and I get tunnel vision.

He doesn't see me at first, as I'm just staring at him, *and her.*

"Audrey, baby, what's wrong?" Hayden asks.

I see him turn his head to what has my attention and his grip on my shoulder tightens slightly.

As Greg and Abby get closer, still unaware of me and Hayden, I fight back the tears. I thought I had cried myself dry, but I guess I was wrong. Why does he affect me like this?

He's an asshole. I know this.

He's a cheater. I deserve better.

He doesn't deserve me. I repeat to myself over and over.

I feel Hayden grab my hand interlocking our fingers and he pulls me up to stand.

"I'm sorry, I think I should go," I finally say, breaking the spell Greg still has me under.

"Oh no you don't, don't let him ruin the fun we're having. Don't let him ruin our night." Hayden's voice is soft and endearing.

I look into his eyes finally and see sympathy. He's not angry at me for ruining our moment. Or upset at my change in demeanor.

"Let's get in line for the Ferris wheel, how does that sound?" he asks as he cups my chin, making sure my full attention is on him.

I don't want the knowledge of Greg being here with *her* to ruin my night. I don't want him to affect me like this anymore. So I nod and smile up at Hayden.

Hayden leaves me for a second to throw our trash away. When he comes back he instantly interlocks our fingers again.

I love the feel of his hold. He's warm. He feels safe. He feels... right.

As he pulls me toward the Ferris wheel I hear the familiar voice call out to me.

EIGHT
Hayden

The sound of this fuckers voice hits my ears and I instantly want to turn around and hit him in the face. Witnesses be damned.

I feel Audrey tense at the sound of her name being called. I stop walking, keeping her hand in mine as we both turn around to face the motherfucker.

I don't know what I thought he would look like but the man that's standing in front of me is exactly it. I can tell when a man is dressed in Daddy's money.

He's in a fucking suit. At a fucking carnival. What a douchebag.

His hair is slicked back with the overuse of hair gel.

Taking him in, my eyes go to the woman he has in his hold.

She's small. Figureless. No curves. Bleach blonde hair. Her face is plastered with makeup and fake eyelashes.

Everything that Audrey is in her simple and natural beauty, this woman is not.

Is this the woman he was cheating on her with? Is she the one he was fucking on Audrey's birthday? Something tells me it's yes to both.

"Hi Greg," Audrey finally says. *Greg*, what a fucking douchebag name!

I can see how small she feels standing a few feet away from him. Did he do this to her? Make her feel small and worthless?

The urge to fucking hit him comes rushing back. Until I feel Audrey squeeze my hand in hers.

Greg sizes me up, and I stand a bit taller. If this fucker wants to step up to me I will greatly oblique.

The look on the face of the woman next to him tells me all I need to know about her. She would leave Greg in a heartbeat if I told her to. No loyalty. If she did she wouldn't have fucked a taken man. Let alone be here with him, knowing Audrey would be here.

I can't help the look of disgust on my face as I watch her look at me.

I don't let this conversation continue as I glare at Greg and his companion.

"If you don't mind, Audrey and I have a Ferris wheel to get on." I don't wait for their response as I turn in place with Audrey and pull her away from that motherfucker.

"You ok?" I ask her as I try to calm my own racing heart and frustration that that man has any effect on her.

She nods yes but her body is tense. I can feel it in the way she holds my hand. How her body is stiff as we walk up to the line, waiting to get on the Ferris wheel.

The line moves at a snail's pace, so I attempt to break her out of her frustration. "What's your favorite thing to do here?"

She lets out a breath before answering, "I love the carnival games and the hayride. Oh, and the food. It's always covered in grease and so good." she laughs.

We begin to move a few feet then stop once more.

"She is nothing compared to you my black cat," I attempt to break her out of the spell he still has her under.

She must know that the new woman he's with is a downgrade to her. It's his loss. He's the idiot in this situation.

"Thank you but I see what she looks like. She might as well be a supermodel." She sounds defeated. Like she's lost in a contest made for one.

Rage starts to build in my stomach as I turn to her. I hold her chin with my hands, forcing her to look me in the eyes.

"Listen to me very carefully Audrey because I'm only going to say this once," my voice coming out a bit harsher than intended but fuck I can't help it.

She's awoken something territorial inside of me. She needs to hear me loud and clear. Her eyes go wide and I can tell she's holding her breath to see what I'm going to say next, "You, my little black cat, are the most beautiful creature I have ever laid my eyes on. She may be pretty by society's standards but all I saw was the ugliness of her heart. You are beautiful in every way."

Her eyes go soft at my words. She may not want to believe me but something tells me she needed to hear the words as much as I wanted to say them.

"Now what do you say we get on this Ferris wheel, and enjoy the rest of our night?" I smile down at her, not wanting to break our contact or this moment we are sharing.

She nods with my hand still holding her chin and we share a small laugh.

A few minutes go by and we make it to the front of the line to the Ferris wheel. We hear the couple behind us say, "that was the scariest thing ever. Wow."

"Yeah, definitely, we *will* be doing that again tonight!" the man says.

I can't help but turn around and ask, "what was scary?"

"Oh man, the new fun house. The floor moves, there are tunnels and things pop out at you. Then at the end, you're left in a pitch black room looking for the exit," the guy says with a look of wonder in his eyes.

I smile at them and turn back to Audrey, "what do you say black cat, wanna explore the fun house tonight?" I nudge her with my shoulder, being playful but all I see on her face is fear.

"Yeah," she says nervously, not even looking at me. Her fear should have me concerned but all it does is turn me on even more with her standing next to me.

Would she want to play in that situation? Would she let me fuck her while she fights me, screams for me? I pray the answer is yes because my cock is hard as steel just at the thought of having her, taking her in that way.

The Ferris wheel slows to allow the group to exit and the worker comes to open the white gate to allow Audrey and I through. We show our bands to him as we step through and walk toward the gondola.

NINE
Audrey

Determined to forget about Greg and Abby for the rest of the night, I step into the gondola that has a lowered base with bar seats on both sides. Colored glass runs around the whole top half of the gondola. A metal umbrella covers the top, shielding us from the outside world.

Hayden steps in taking the seat opposite me, locking us in from the inside. His eyes are firmly on me and he doesn't say a word. But his eyes tell me everything I need to know.

He hates Greg for ruining our night just as much as I do. "I'm sorry," I say looking at him, "I don't want to ruin the rest of your night with my sour mood. If you want to go back to your friend after this," I'm stopped mid-sentence as he held up his hand.

As he does the Ferris wheel starts to move pushing us toward the sky. We stop every few feet to allow more people to get on and off. Hayden and I don't say anything as we reach the top and stay there.

I look through the glass out onto the town square below us. The crowds of people walking around, eating food, playing carnival games. Enjoying their night.

I *was* enjoying my night until Greg showed his stupid face. Pushing my hatred for him even further down, I look back to Hayden who hasn't changed his facial expression since we got on this ride.

I've ruined his night. I know it. He knows it. He's just biding his time until this ride is over and he'll leave as soon as the ride is over.

The ride starts up again, this time not stopping sending us back down in one motion.

"Audrey," Hayden finally says. But this time when I look at him I don't see frustration, I see... something darker.

He leans closer to me, and without thinking I lean in closer as well, until our faces are inches apart.

"I hate that he affects you like this. You are wasting your time even thinking about him. Let me show you how a man needs to treat you." He cups my face into his hand.

His touch sets a fire in the pit of my stomach and the butterflies from the corn maze come to life again.

"Please" I moan out, unashamed of my want for this man. I am lost in my need for Hayden at this moment.

My plea springs him into motion as he leans back into the back of the gondola, he spreads his legs wide. The bulge in his pants is noticed and appreciated by the wetness that's building in my panties.

"Lean back for me black cat," he demands. His eyes are piercing into me as I do as I'm told.

My back hits the cold metal. A stark contrast to my body temperature.

ONE NIGHT WITH MY NEIGHBOR

"Spread your legs, baby," again I do as he asks. I don't think, I just do.

With my legs spread wide, Hayden licks his lips as his eyes leave mine, traveling down my body. With every inch lower his eyes go, I feel his gaze. It's red hot.

"Pull your skirt up, let me see that fine pussy,"

I hesitate for a second, but in that second Hayden's eyes are on me, with one eyebrow raised.

I start to gather up the material at my hips. The fabric rises inch by inch. Hayden adjusts himself as the material goes up my body. Until it's all bunched up at my hips. The cool night air hits my bare legs, cooling my rising body temperature.

I wait for his next instruction but he doesn't say anything. All he does is sit across from me with his legs wide, his dick twitching in his pants as he forces air into his lungs.

Pride fills my chest at the realization that I have this effect on him. He's hot and turned on because of me. I've done this to him. Me and my body that he is salivating over.

A second goes by before he leaves his seat and is on his knees between my legs. His eyes haven't left the area between my legs as I watch him.

His warm touch starts at my ankles and snakes its way up my legs until they are on my thighs. His fingers twitch with anticipation as he taps them at a rapid pace on my thighs.

"Can I taste you?" he asks and I agree without hesitation.

His hands go to my hips and with one tug he rips off my panties. I gasp in shock but the wetness between my legs continues to build.

"Let's see if I can make you come before this ride is over, what do you say black cat?" he grunts out.

"Please," I breathe out, unable to form any more words than that. Not that I would because as soon as I beg, his warm lips are between my legs.

A single soft lick has my legs going weak. He pulls away and smiles up at me with his dark eyes.

"You taste as sweet as you look at my little black cat. Now sit back and enjoy while I devour this cunt." he grunts out with a devilish smile.

So I do as I'm told and lean back against the cold metal of the gondola and let him do just that.

His tongue starts soft and slow but with the seconds going by he picks up his pace and roughness. I have no other choice but to look up at the night sky. The see-through umbrella covering lets me enjoy the cloudless cool night.

I can feel his tongue enter me over and over. And without notice, he bites down on my clit. I scream out uncontrollably. Ashamed I cover my mouth, praying and hoping no one around us can see or hear us.

Hayden grabs at my hand and pulls his lips away from my pussy and says, "don't you dare muffle your pleasure. I want to hear you scream when I make you come."

He's merciless with his tongue and teeth. It has never felt like this before. Even with my toys at home.

I'm helpless when it comes to his touch on me. I can feel him everywhere. From my toes to the top of my head. His voice echoed in my ear, praising me over and over.

"That's my good little kitten, let me hear you," is the last thing he says before the stars in the sky explode. Bright lights invade my vision. My scream vibrates throughout my body.

I don't care who can hear me. My orgasms have never felt like this. But Hayden doesn't stop. He licks and bites me through my orgasm. Dragging it out.

I look at him as he's still kneeling between my legs. I can see the aftermath of my orgasm shining on his lips. He runs his tongue along his lips and he smiles up at me.

ONE NIGHT WITH MY NEIGHBOR

He leans back, grabs my skirt, and lets it fall back down onto the ground. "Sweet as honey, addicting like heroin," he says just as our gondola comes to a stop and the worker comes to unlatch our door to let us out.

TEN
Hayden

I don't think I'll ever get enough of Audrey. This interesting night we are having can't end here. I'm instantly addicted and want her in every way.

I fingered her in the corn maze and now have eaten her out on the Ferris wheel. But I want more. I need more. My body vibrates with the need to fill her. To own her.

The post-orgasmic haze is still in her eyes as I take her hand and lead her out of the gondola and make our way through the crowd back onto solid ground.

I know she just got out of a relationship with Greg but would she be willing to start something with me so soon afterward? Would she let me fuck the memory of Greg out of her?

Just the thought of that fucker touching her or having her in the way I long for, makes my blood boil. How could he cheat on someone as perfect as Audrey?

But I can't help but smile at the thought that his loss is my gain. But only if she's willing to have me. I don't want to rush her. I want to take anything she is willing to give me.

"Where to now kitten?" I say as I walk us to a part of the sidewalk that isn't so crowded.

She doesn't answer me. Her eyes are glazed over. The smile plastered on her face lets me know she's slowly still coming out of her orgasm high. I internally pat myself on the back.

This is just the beginning for us little black cat.

"Audrey?" I grab at her shoulders, breaking her out of her trance.

She looks up at me, "huh what did you say?"

I can't help but laugh. "That good huh?"

Her cheeks turn an embarrassing shade of red as I smile at her and she tries to hide her face from me.

"Oh no, you don't," I gently grab her chin and pull it back toward me so she doesn't have a choice but to look at me. "Don't be embarrassed with how good that was. Let yourself enjoy it."

She nods with understanding as she says, "thank you, it's never felt like that before. It was..." She tries to find the right word.

"Amazing," I jumped in.

"Yeah, amazing," she smiles up at me. Her laugh is bright and full of joy.

And in this moment I promise to always make her laugh just like that. "Now that we've settled that, where would you like to go now?"

I step aside to stand next to her, allowing her to take in everything around us. Her head goes side to side taking it all in. To our left are the food trucks, then the corn maze. In the corner, is the fun house.

I mentally take a note to make sure to take her to that before the night is over.

Between us and the courthouse are three rows of carnival games. From kid-friendly games like throwing darts at balloons and ring toss, to more adult fun games shooting metal cans and 3-point basketball shots.

"Can we go play some games?" she asks in an almost whisper.

"Of course we can kitten," I grab her hand, missing her touch, and lead her toward the games.

As we walk through the crowd I ask, "what do you want to play first?"

Again she's looking at all the games. After a few steps, we walk up to a throwing game.

"This one," she points and the worker walks up to explain the game. He tells us it's ten dollars for three attempts.

I try to hide my annoyance at the highway robbery that is carnival games. Nonetheless, my kitten wants me to play and win her something so I will.

I take my wallet from my back pocket, fish out a ten-dollar bill, and hand it to the worker. He hands me three softball-sized white balls and tells me that I can win a prize from the first row if I make all three shots.

The row is lined with small stuffed animals. "What do I need to do to win one of those?" I ask, pointing to the top row of life-size stuffed animals.

He tells me I need to make all three plus three more. Without question, I hand him another ten-dollar bill and he gives me three more balls.

With determination running through my veins, I look down at Audrey who is eyeing me with something I'm not used to seeing.

Pride.

I grab one of the balls from the wooden stand in front of me, rolling it in my hand as I position myself to throw.

I pull my arm back and throw the ball with full force. It flies out of my hand and goes through the hole a few feet away with ease.

A smile rises on my face and I can hear Audrey cheer. She's smiling up at me as she claps her hands.

I unapologetically watch as her boobs bounce with every small jump she makes cheering me on. My dick comes to life again instantly.

With lust filled determination running through me, I grab the next two balls and throw them one after another. Both fly through their intended target.

Audrey cheers after each one. She grabs my arm after the third ball lands. Rising to her tip toes she kisses me on the cheek.

Her kiss is warm, and comforting, and edges me on to win that top prize for her.

As I pick up the fourth ball, a crowd starts to form. Cheers start to roar as I sink the fourth ball and instantly pick up the fifth ball. It goes flying, it hits the edge of the hole but falls to the other side.

Loud cheers erupt but I look at Audrey who must be in a state of shock. Her eyes are large and she's covering her mouth with both her hands.

I grab the sixth and final ball. Holding it in my hand I look down at Audrey.

"Kiss for good luck?" I smile at her.

She doesn't hesitate as she rises on her tiptoes and goes for my cheek. But I turn my head just in time and take her lips into mine.

My tongue invades her mouth, cupping her face with my free hand. Seconds, minutes, hours, or days must go by before I break our kiss. Her cheeks are flushed and she laughs out a nervous laugh.

Not breaking eye contact with her as I lean my hand back and swing through, releasing the ball.

I don't watch as the ball goes flying out of my hand.

I don't watch as it tumbles through the air between us and the target.

I don't even watch as it rolls through the target, dead center.

What I do watch is Audrey holding her breath. The way her eyes go wide with anticipation as the ball leaves my hand. The way she takes in a breath as it flies closer to the target. I even watch as she gasps as the ball rolls through the hole landing on the other side.

As if in slow motion, she turns to me with a starry eyed look on her face. She screams with excitement, wrapping her hands around my neck.

The crowd's cheers are muffled as I can't concentrate on anything but the feel of her body against mine. She and I are alone in a swarm of people.

My hands wrap around her waist, holding her in place and the worker comes up to us. "Congratulations, pick any prize on the top row."

Without hesitation, I point to the prize I have been eyeing since starting this silly game.

ELEVEN
Audrey

The people around us are cheering as Hayden just landed the final shot to win one of the grand prizes.

Without releasing me Hayden looks at the worker and points to one of the prizes hanging above us.

I follow the length of his arm to the tip of his finger until my eyes are on the large black cat stuffed animal.

Unable to hide my amusement, I tighten my hold around Hayden's neck. His firm grip around my waist holds me inches off the ground. But a part of me wishes he would never let me go.

The worker takes a long metal stick from the corner of his game stand and brings it above his head. He unhooks the stuffed animal and brings it in front of us.

Hayden sets me down, looks at me, and smiles. Telling me without words to take the prize.

I feel silly with how much joy is coursing through me. No one has ever won anything like this for me before. Let alone something this big.

Wrapping my hands around the life sized soft black cat stuffed animal I can't help but smile up at Hayden.

He smiles back at me with a soft childlike smile. But it's his eyes that are filled with something not so soft. Something primal.

"Thank you," I say to the worker, as Hayden and I turn toward the crowd and start to walk away.

As we walk side by side, my happiness instantly dies when I see him. Greg.

The scowl that's plastered on his face tells me everything I need to know.

It's not anger, it's jealousy.

But what would he be jealous of? I was always the one to drag him to these things. He never had fun, let alone played any of the carnival games to win me anything.

Hayden must sense my slight change in demeanor. He wraps one of his hands around my shoulder, leaning me closer to his body. I feel his soft lips on my temple and I can't help but feel like the luckiest girl in all of Hollow Creek.

Not paying Greg and Abby any mind, Hayden and I make our way to the sidewalk. I can feel their eyes still on us and Hayden leads me further away.

We walk through the crowd with my prize on my hip and Hayden's hand in mine. This feels normal.

It feels good.

It feels right.

But we couldn't possibly make us a thing. He told me tonight was just one night of rule breaking fun. Fun to help me get over Greg.

I can say with one hundred percent certainty that I am over Greg. But would Hayden want more? Would he want to extend whatever this is? Whatever we are, to more than just tonight.

We continue walking and I get lost in my own doubt when Hayden stops walking. The sudden stop breaks me out of my haze as I notice the row of small shops.

The shop in front of us had brown paper covering the windows.

A large sign in one of the windows says "Coming Soon" in big red letters.

Underneath that it says, "Midnight Tattoos"

"What is this," I ask, looking up at Hayden.

"This is the tattoo shop that my friend and I are opening soon." I notice him straighten his back and he stands a few inches taller. Pride is written all over his features.

"That's amazing. When are you opening?"

"Hopefully soon, if all the permits go through. We're having a grand opening next month if everything goes to plan."

"That's amazing," I repeat.

"Wanna see it?" he asks, looking down at me with a bright smile that reaches his eyes.

"Yes!" not hiding my excitement.

He reaches into his back pocket and takes out a ring of keys. Shuffling through them he takes a black key between his fingers and unlocks both locks on the glass door.

Opening the door, he holds out his hand and leads me through the threshold. Closing the door behind us and locking it again, I stand in place as he walks over to the corner and turns the lights on.

A large open area comes to life. The walls are a cream color, covered with frames of artwork. A small L-shaped desk sits in the corner where I assume the checkout is.

The rest of the area is a section with half walls to divide the stations for the tattoo artists. The walls are just high enough to give privacy but low enough if they want to talk to each other.

He takes my prize from him and sets it on the counter. Hayden takes my hand and leads me through the aisle between the two sides of the stations. As we walk through I notice some areas are empty whereas others are personalized with things.

As we make it to the back he stops at the last two stations and turns to face me. He looks to his left and says, "this is my station."

I turn my head and take in all the artwork. His section of the wall is covered with black and white pieces. From large intricate pieces like a pirate ship in the ocean to small detailed pieces like a bouquet of flowers no bigger than a half dollar.

"Did you draw all these?" I turn back to face him. He doesn't say anything but just nods. I walk further into his space running my hands along the desk that's filled with bottles of different colored inks and supplies still in their wrappings.

"Does it hurt?" I ask.

Where Hayden is covered with art, my body is blemish free. Nothing stands out about me.

"Depends," he says, stepping into the space behind me. "Depends where you get it, how much detail is in it, and if you use certain colors or not." he elaborates as his hands land on my shoulders.

I turn in place to face him. I tip my head back to look him in the eyes. Those stormy eyes center my racing heart.

Taking a single step back, I lift my shirt to expose my hip bone. "What if I got something," I try to sound sexy and seductive as I run my hand to my hip and tap on it. "Here,"

He takes a sharp breath and I watch as his Adam's apple bobs up and down. His eyes darken as he licks his lips and says, "it wouldn't hurt too bad."

His voice sounds strained like he's fighting his desperation for me. I like affecting him like this. I like knowing my body does this to him.

"What would you get?" he grunts out, closing the space between us.

"I was thinking," I look up at him, "a small black cat." I run both my hands up his arms with the faintest touch, until I get to his shoulders, along his collarbone, then up his neck until I cup his cheeks.

TWELVE
Hayden

I didn't plan on bringing her here. But a part of me wanted to show her what I've been working on since moving to this fucking town.

This shop is months, shit years, of hard work. A tattoo shop has always been our dream, and we are so close to it being a reality.

The only thing holding us up is some stupid permit paperwork with the city.

We passed out flyers with our grand opening date plastered on them. There is no going back. We will look like jokes if this doesn't work out.

I pray everything goes through and we can finally open our doors.

But having Audrey here, in my shop, in my space sets a new desire in motion. I want to have her, in every way.

Visions of her naked in my workspace, in my chair, against the wall of framed artwork flood my mind. I would have to spend hours sanitizing my station but something tells me it would all be worth it.

When she brought up getting a tattoo, a possessiveness I've never felt creeps up into my chest.

I will be the only one to ever touch this body, to see it in its full form. I want to brand her, to permanently pierce her skin with my ink and tattoo gun.

Will she scream in pain or settle into the numbing pleasure only a tattoo can bring?

Then she said she wanted a black cat, of all fucking things, on her hip bone. Who knew the simple exposure of her hip bone would have me salivating like a starving dog?

Her hands cup my cheeks as we stand toe to toe, only the air we're breathing between us.

"I can do that for you baby," I exhale the breath I was holding. "But right now all I want to do is devour these luscious lips of yours,"

A smile forms on her face and her eyes light up with excitement. Giving me the green light I was waiting for from her.

Our lips crash into each other. My hands can't touch enough of her body. My fingers grab a handful of her hair, breaking our kiss as I lean her head back.

She's breathless as I stare into her eyes. "Your lips are sweet, your pussy like honey. Is my kitten sweet all over?"

She moans into my touch. With my hand still holding her head back I plant kisses along her chin starting at her ear and then making my way down her neck.

More moans fill the room as she says my name, "Hayden, please,"

"Oh kitten, you can beg better than that," I stop mid kiss on her exposed collar bone. I love toying with her. Getting her to speak out her wants and desires.

"Hayden please, keep kissing me. You feel so good." She's fighting to catch her breath as I continue to kiss her.

As I make it further down her chest, I kiss each breast through the fabric of her shirt and bra. Wanting a taste, I release her hair from my grasp and expose both her breasts.

Her nipples are pink and hard. I run the faintest touch with my fingers along the rim of her nipples.

"Oh my god," Audrey moans even louder. "Hayden, yes please,"

With one hand working her nipple with the smallest of pressure, I lean down and take the other into my mouth. Letting my tongue piercing do most of the work.

Repeating my motion between my hand on one breast and my mouth on the other, I look up at her and throw my eyelashes.

Her head is thrown back in bliss as she loses herself in the feel of me touching her.

My tongue circles her nipple over and over until I take it between my teeth and softly bite it at the same time as I pinch her other nipple with my fingers.

She doesn't moan, she screams into the open space, ringing in my ears.

Her legs give out and we both fall to the ground.

My legs lay crisscrossed out in front of me, and she is straddled on top of me. We let the silence settle between us.

"That was," her head falls onto my chest and she lets out a laugh. "Is it always like that?" she asks, still hiding her face from me.

I run my hands on her back and say, "if it's done right, yes."

A few minutes pass as we stay like this, interlocked in one another. I don't want to get up, I don't want to break this moment between us.

She breaks the silence when she says, "let's go see what else there is to do."

I agree with a soft pat on her ass, signaling for her to stand. "let's go,"

She stands and I follow. I watch as she readjusts herself back into her shirt. She does a cute little shimmy resetting her outfit. Running her hands through her hair, setting the soft black curls back into place.

I adjust myself as well, desperately trying to hide my hard cock. When we're both ready, we look at each other and laugh at the same time. Her laugh is soft and full of joy.

If I could bottle up this moment and sell it I would. I want to live in this moment forever. Everything and everyone else be damned. This moment right now, will live in my mind forever.

Her bright smile. Her flushed cheeks. The long strands of black curls. Plump perky breasts. Her full figure. The long firm legs that house her perfect pussy. Audrey is perfect. I hope in the few hours that we've spent together and the few hours we have left, I show her just how much.

I hold out my hand between us pleading with her to take it. I don't have to wait long because she instantly takes it and I lead us back to the front of the store.

She goes to grab her bag and the stuffed animal I won her, but I hold her in place. "Leave them, you can pick them up in the morning," I say.

At the mention of tomorrow, her eyes go wide in suspicion. Has she thought about seeing me after tonight? Does she want to or is this just a one-night thing to get over her fucking cheating ex?

"Tomorrow," she says matter-of-factly, and I can't help but smile at her.

"Tomorrow," I state, pulling her into my hold once more and walking us out of my shop. I lock the store behind me and we make our way down the sidewalk once more.

"Where to now, kitten," I ask as we continue down the packed sidewalk.

"What about the fun house," she answers, pointing to the large metal contraption a few yards away.

"Funhouse it is, let's go," picking up our pace slightly as we work our way through the crowd.

THIRTEEN
Audrey

As we make our way down the sidewalk toward the fun house I can't help but settle my body into Haydens'. His arm is draped over my shoulder pulling me into him.

Warmth fills me, as it has all night. The feeling of comfort takes over me.

When he asked me to leave my bag and stuffed animal at his shop and we would pick them up tomorrow, my chest filled with anticipation.

Just the thought of seeing Hayden after tonight has me smiling like a love sick puppy.

Maybe whatever we're doing tonight we can explore more of. Together. With him opening up a tattoo shop in the center of town, it means he has plans of staying long term.

Which means either way I'd be seeing him around town. Whether we run into each other at the grocery store or around town, Hayden is now a permanent future in my life.

And I don't have any issues with that.

What if he gets sick of you just like Greg did? The old me creeps up. Everything was great with Greg at first. We had fun and enjoyed each other.

Would Hayden get bored of me? Would he use me and then throw me away like yesterday's trash? Will I eventually catch him cheating on me one day?

The sickening thoughts have me faltering my steps.

"Audrey, you ok?" Hayden's voice feels so far away as I let the intrusive thoughts take over my mind.

I look up at him, I watch his mouth move but nothing is hitting my ears. Can I handle continuing this amazing night with this man and just walking away?

Walking away, ending it, then running into him all over town.

My heart breaks at the thought. Just in the few hours I've spent with him, I've become full of need and want for this man.

I know everyone after him will fall short. There will only ever be one Hayden. Everyone else won't be worth my time. I know it deep down in my gut. He has ruined me for everyone else.

But I can't tell him that. I can't ruin whatever this is. This is just one night of fun for him. He will wake up in the morning and think nothing of what this night meant to me.

I feel my body being pulled and I don't fight it. I know wherever he is taking me, I will blindly follow.

Am I stupid for being this attached to someone I just met? Probably, but there is something safe in Hayden that my soul is crying out for.

He leads me into an alley and I feel the hard brick scratch at my back as he cages me in with his hands on either side of my shoulders.

I can't look at him so I do what I've always done with Greg, I plant my eyesight onto the ground.

"Audrey, look at me."

I don't. It's the first time all night I haven't done what he has asked of me almost instantly.

"Audrey, Look. At. Me." he grunts out each word.

"I can't," I'm trying to hold back the tears that are fighting to break free from the corners of my eyes.

"Audrey, baby, please look at me." Now he's the one that sounds broken and weak.

I slowly raise my head to meet his gaze. Pain is written all over his face as he studies me. His eyes run all over my face, taking me in fully.

It's when his eyes land back on mine that the dam breaks. A single tear falls from my eye then another and another. I lift my hand to swipe them away but he beats me to it.

The pad of his thumb runs along my cheek, catching the tears. "Audrey, talk to me. What's wrong?"

How do I come up with the words without sounding stupid and pitiful? How do I explain in the short few hours we've spent together that I've become attached to him in more than a physical way?

I know I'll sound crazy but that doesn't stop me, "I don't want us to end after tonight. I don't want this to be just a one time thing. I don't," I don't finish my train of thought as another tear falls.

"Oh baby, this was never going to be just a one night thing," he states with a weak smile looking down at me. As he swipes the other tear, his hand stays cupped on my chin.

"You can't and won't be getting rid of me any time soon. You are my kitten. Get used to it." He says running his thumb along my cheek is the softest of touches.

"What if," I don't mean to speak my intensive thoughts out into the world but they hang between us.

Hayden's eyes narrow in confusion as he thinks about what I'm trying to say. I wish I could take the words back. Take back the past five minutes.

"Never mind," I try my hardest to get past this tense moment. I fake a smile and go to step, but his hands don't move.

"Let's get a few things straight Audrey. I am not Greg," he says. And I know that. He has proven more than once that he is, in fact *not* Greg. but the fear of the what-ifs has me questioning everything.

Nothing hurts more than knowing you've wasted ten years with someone just to have your heart ripped in two.

If I look back at the time I spent with Greg I can point out all the red flags. They were bright neon colored, flashing big warning lights.

"I know," I whisper, fighting back the tears once more.

"Then you should know that I would never treat you how you've told me he has treated you. I will treat you like the queen that you are. You deserve to be worshiped and taken care of."

I stare into his eyes. The emotion in them tells me he's telling the truth.

When I would look into Greg's eyes and he would tell me one thing, I could tell deep in the backs of his eyes that he was lying. Another red flag.

I trust Hayden when he says he's not Greg. Every fiber in my body believes him. I trust him when he says he'll take care of me. I need and want them more than he knows.

"I trust you," I say my thoughts into existence. His eyes fill with an emotion I'm not familiar with. They are soft and hard at the same time. As if he's fighting something deep inside of himself.

I know now that I wholeheartedly trust Hayden. Whatever this is between, I have no doubt I would go where he leads me.

Without a second thought. I trust him to take care of me. Trust him to please me. To love me.

Love. Is what that feeling feels like? Is this what it's meant to be like?

In the ten years I was with Greg, it took him years to say the words. I fight to not say them to Hayden at this moment.

It's too soon. It's been a few hours.

He pulls his hands off the brick wall, releasing me from the figurative cage he had me in, "now what do you say when we enjoy the rest of our night,"

I smile up at him and take his hand into mine. He leads me out of the alley and toward the fun house.

FOURTEEN
Hayden

Love is an emotion I haven't had the luxury to feel towards a whole lot of people.

I never felt it from my mother, when I begged her to spend time with me. Not toward my father who I desperately wanted to find something, anything, in common with. But they were too busy making millions, so I was left to the nannies.

But the emotion I feel toward Audrey in this moment feels like more. More than lust. Though I do love the feel of her body falling apart in mine.

What is it called when you are so overwhelmed with a person, that the thought of losing them leaves a soul crushing ache in the pit of your stomach?

She's worried that I'll do something to hurt her. As if I ever could.

I worry that when she inevitably realizes she deserves better than me, I won't survive her leaving me.

As I lead her toward the fun house, I tighten my grip on her interlocked fingers in mine. Wanting, needing her to feel the ache that's in my heart for her.

The ache of wanting more with her. I need her in my life. Praying she never realized just how much more she deserves than me.

I am nothing in her presence. I don't deserve to be spending these few hours with her. But I will take them and cherish them for what they are. A life altering event that has set my life in a new direction.

As we make it to the end of the short line, I bring our connected hands up to my mouth and kiss the back of her hand.

Smiling down at her as she smiles up at me, I'm refilled with happiness unlike anything before.

"Stay here, I'll be right back," I say, releasing her hand from mine as an idea comes to my head. Confusion is written all over her face as I leave her in line.

I make my way toward the worker at the front gate of the funhouse. Big red and orange colored bulbs flash bright, spelling out the word "fun house."

The entrance is painted with clowns with wicked smiles on their faces. A haunted house is painted in the corner. Bats and cobwebs all over.

"Hey man," I say to the worker who lets a couple of kids through the entrance. "Can I ask a favor?"

He eyes me suspiciously. I know he's had a long night already and it's only going to get longer. He doesn't want to hear what I have to say. He doesn't get paid enough to care.

I reach for the wallet, I need him to care. "Do you see that girl that's in the back of the line," I turn to look at Audrey who's eyeing me suspiciously.

"Yeah," I can't miss the annoyed tone in his voice.

"What would it cost to let us be the only ones through this fun house for a few minutes?" I ask, opening my wallet and taking out the cash I have.

The man looks at me with his eyebrows raised. His eyes go from me to the stack of cash now in my hands.

"How's two hundred sounds?" I count out two hundred dollars in my twenties, slowly.

"Five," he says in a whisper, looking around to see if anyone is listening to our semi-private conversation.

"$250," I rebut playfully. I don't think he understands how much I am willing to pay for this moment of complete privacy with Audrey.

"Four," he spits back with a smile.

"Three," I said right back.

He eyes me suspiciously as if he's being tested on a hidden camera. His eyes go side to side making sure no one is looking at us as he says, "deal."

I count out $300 in twenties, fold it in half, and hand him the bundle of cash with a smile. "We can wait in line so you can let the rest of these people through. But we are the last ones to go in until we come out, understood?"

He nods his head in understanding and pockets the cash quickly as if he doesn't it'll disappear.

I turn and make my way back to Audrey who is staring at me with concern. My plan is in motion, we just have to get through the next few minutes in line before I can have my way with her.

I take her hand back into mine without a word and stand facing forward. I can feel her looking at me as we step a few steps forward as the line moves up.

"What was all that about?" she asks.

"Just needed to have a little chat with the worker," is all I say because if I say anything else, it would be a lie. I don't want to ruin the surprise I have planned for her.

For us.

"Tell me more about yourself Audrey," wanting to change the subject.

She looks up at me and then back toward the front of the line. Without looking back at me she says, "you were right," she takes a deep breath.

"Right about what?" I ask, needing to know.

"At the beginning of the night, when you said I was a good girl. I am." She forces out as if she's ashamed of the memories running through her mind.

I don't speak, letting her take her time explaining herself.

"I was the girl that got good grades and was never late to class. Got honor roll, and never stayed out past my ridiculous curfew. I went to college and got my degree, all to make my parents proud." She pauses and her cheeks turn red, not from embarrassment but from frustration.

"But it never mattered because it was never good enough. There was always someone out there that did better. Someone who got the better grades, the better scholarship. Tonight has been the first night in my life that I've been able to truly enjoy myself."

She's fighting her emotions again. I see the sparkle of tears starting to build in the corners of her eyes. And she continues, "thank you Hayden, for tonight for everything."

I bring her hand in mine to my mouth again and kiss the back of her hand. I don't stop there, I kiss each knuckle. Then I kiss the underside of her wrist and she must like that because she lets out a small whimper.

"You are more than welcome kitten, but the night is still young and I have so much more fun planned for us." I give her a devilish smile. She smiles back knowingly.

She may not know the full plan that's forming in my head but she can't deny that whatever I'm going to do to her, she is going to enjoy it.

The line has moved up until Audrey and I are the next couple to go. I look at the worker and wink at him.

He walks out from his little control panel. "I'm so sorry ladies and gentlemen but this ride needs to be shut down for maintenance. We hope to have it ready in a few minutes."

The line behind us grunts out their frustration and they start to walk away. Audrey starts to pull us out of line but I don't move.

I look down at her and wink, setting her back into place next to me. I watch as the line behind us walks away and the worker eyes me suspiciously.

He slowly starts to open the metal gate to let Audrey and me through.

"Come Kitten, let's have some fun." I look back at her. She smiles and follows me without another word shared. I shake the worker's hand as I lead Audrey through the fabric into the fun house.

FIFTEEN
Audrey

When the fun house worker announced that it would be shutting down for maintenance, I got a little upset.

The fun house was always a favorite of mine throughout the years. The shifting floors, flashing lights, even the mirror maze that led to an open area that was pitch black and you had to find your way to the exit.

It always added a bit of fun heart pounding excitement to my night in the past. So I was upset when he said it was closing.

But Hayden didn't move, he stayed in line. While everyone around us walked away, Hayden kept himself and me there.

I was confused and concerned at first. But when I looked at Hayden and the way he looked at the worker I knew he did something.

He planned something and I'm now willingly following. With our hands interlocked together he pulls me through the fabric at the entrance. The bright lights and sounds of the outside instantly fade as we walk through.

He stops walking and turns to face me. Though in the dim light of the fun house, I can't make out much of his features. But I can feel his hand in mine and his other hand running up my spine.

"Do you trust me?" Hayden asks and I answer without hesitation.

"Yes," knowing I do. Wholeheartedly.

"Do you want to have some fun?" he leans down and whispers in my ear. His breath on my neck sends hot molten lava down my spine straight to my pussy.

"Yes," I say without question. I want whatever he has planned. If it's anything like what I experienced with him earlier tonight, then I want it all.

"Follow me," he whispers as he turns around and starts to walk away. I blindly follow.

I have to keep my hands along the narrow wall, going off of memory from past years of what to expect. The floor beneath me starts to slide forward and backward.

Keeping my balance I walk a few feet until I'm on more solid ground. I let out a gleeful laugh.

"Hayden," I speak into the darkness.

"I'm right in front of you baby, keep walking, come to me," he says. His voice feels so far away but at the same time, it's as if he's right next to me.

Even though I can barely make out what's right in front of me, I can feel Hayden all over me.

Though he is what feels like miles away, I feel him on my skin. I feel him everywhere. His hand is tangled in my hair. His touch on my neck, hands, and hips. He's invaded every inch of my skin without even being close by.

As I make my way further into the fun house, a rainbow of lights starts to strobe. My vision adjusts just in time as I walk into what feels like a brick wall.

ONE NIGHT WITH MY NEIGHBOR

"Oh my god," I scream out.

Strong hands hold my shoulders. Hot breath reaches my spine as I hear, "ready to play kitten?"

His voice echoes in my ears as I nod. But knowing my nod won't be enough for him, I say, "yes, I'm ready."

"That's my good girl." he leads me through the tunnel of techo colored lights.

With my hand in his, he leads me to the mirror maze that I knew was coming. No matter how many times in the past I've done mazes, I always seem to run into a mirror a time or two.

"Ready?" He smiles at me. I straighten my spine, nod my head, and smile back at him.

Letting go of my hand, he starts to walk through the maze, I watch him trying my hardest to remember every turn he makes.

It's no use, I can't seem to concentrate on his movements. I'm more interested in his strong broad shoulders. His firm legs with every step he makes. Everything about him seems to turn me on.

When he makes it to the other end, I start to make my way through the maze. I use my hands against the mirrors to see when there is a gap for me to walk through.

With his eyes following me, the wetness in between can't be ignored. Our eyes are locked on one another. Slowly I make it to the end with a laugh and smile.

"Good job kitten, how the real fun begins," Hayden smirks down at me. He steps to the side and opens the curtain for me to work through.

I know what comes next. The pitch black room. I remember the couple from earlier talking about it when we were in line at the Ferris wheel.

I step into the blackness and once again my vision goes. I can't make out anything in the room. Everything is covered in darkness.

"Hayden," I whisper out.

Nothing. No reply.

"Hayden," I say again, a little bit louder. I wait a second to see if I can feel him around me.

"I'm right here baby," he says, scaring me. I jump as I turn around and hold out my hands in front of me to grab hold of him.

I don't see anything or feel anything. He's nowhere. But he feels as though he's everywhere.

"Take off your panties baby," I hear him. He feels so far away. But regardless, I do as I'm told.

With shaky hands, I reach under my skirt, grab my panties, and slide them down my legs.

"Hold them in front of you," Hayden says, and again I do as I'm told.

As soon as I hold my hand out with my panties in them, I feel his warm touch run along my arm to the tip of my fingers.

The touch of him melts the chill I'm feeling between my legs. He takes my panties from me. I don't see him but I hear him take in a loud breath.

"Oh kitten, your panties are soaked. You're ready for me already." His tone is laced with need and want.

My brain misfires, and I can't seem to speak. The words are stuck in my throat.

"I've waited all night to fuck you, I think now is as good a time as any, what do you think?" His voice is all around me, I can feel him circling me.

"Please," is all I'm able to force out of my lips. I have lost the ability to form thoughts. He has taken over everything. My body, my thoughts, my rational thinking.

I'm his and he seems to know it. He's toying with me and I'm his willing plaything, at this moment.

"Beg me kitten. Beg me to fuck you. Beg me to take what we both know is mine. What will always be mine." his voice turns harsh. He's fighting his willpower to overtake me at this moment, just as much as I am fighting mine.

I find my voice at that moment. "Please Hayden. Please fuck me. I want you to fuck me. I've wanted it all night. You're all I want. Please." I pant out, giving him and myself exactly what we want at this moment.

SIXTEEN
Hayden

The way she begs has my dick hardening to a painful level. What I would do to be able to see her face at this moment?

This whole night seems to have been leading us here. To this moment. This pitch black room, where it's just her and I.

"You beg so pretty kitten. I'm so hard just from hearing you beg." I grunt out. Even though we are in the pitch black, my vision has slightly adjusted to where I can almost see her full features.

I'm standing right in front of her, where I assume we are in the middle of the darkened room. Nothing but four walls around us.

I hear her gasp. I know from past play times, that her face would turn a deep shade of red with embarrassment. I smile knowing that if the lights were on, that's what I would see.

"Wanna feel me, baby. Wanna feel how hard you've made me?" I ask her as I start to run my hands over her body. Her full hips, arms, and the fullness of her breasts.

"Yes," she finally moans out as if the words were trapped in her throat.

In the darkness, I run my hand down her arm again. I take her open hand in mind and pull it to my chest.

I run her hand from my chest, down to my abs then to where the seam of my shirt meets my belt buckle.

I stop there, subconsciously preparing the both of us for what this will feel like. I have wanted her hands on my dick all night. It's been in the back of my mind since I laid eyes on her just a few hours ago.

A second ticks by and I continue to run her hand further down. I can feel and hear her breathe the lower I go.

Without stopping I guide her hand to my zipper and then toward my high. My dick is rock hard and forms a crease in my pants.

Simultaneously we both grunt out. My dick twitches with appreciation of her touch through my pants.

"Hayden," she moans out.

"On your knees baby," I grunt out. Without seeing her, I know she's falling to her knees in front of me.

"Reach out and undo my zipper." I feel her hands run along my thighs, trying to blindly find my belt buckle.

She fumbles with my belt buckle until it's unclasped. The echo of my zipper comes next. She feels my dick through the thin fabric of my underwear. Her long nails run along the thick shaft until she reaches my tip.

I moan aggressively into the empty room. "Baby, if you don't stop, I'm going to come right now."

She laughs as she pulls her hand away. I instantly miss the touch of her on me.

I work my dick free from my underwear and hold it right in front of where I assume her face would be, "be my good little kitten and suck on my cock."

Her hands go out in front of her, feeling where to put her mouth. I hiss at the feel of her hands on my dick. I don't know how long I will last with my dick in her mouth if this is how she makes me feel with just her touch.

Seconds tick by before I feel something at the tip of my dick. Her tongue is warm and wet. She circles my tip over and over. Precum is already coating it from my need for this woman.

I can't help out the grunt that escapes from my mouth. I know she's smiling because she lets out a faint laugh.

Another second goes by before I feel her tongue again. But this time she doesn't stop the tip. She grabs my dick at the base, raises it, and licks it from base to tip.

My knees are starting to give out with the feel of her tongue on me. She doesn't stop at the tip, she works her outstretched tongue around my tip.

"Oh baby, that feels so good," I praise her. "Take it all for me."

She doesn't need any more motivation than that. I inhale a breath as she takes me all the way to the back of her throat. I groan and she pulls back in a gasp.

"That's it baby, do that again." I put my hand through her hair in praise.

Another breath passes between us until she takes me into her mouth again. But this time, she doesn't stop. Her lips wrap around my shaft fully.

Over and over she sucks my dick. I can feel the wetness build the longer she does it.

My head falls back in pleasure as her muffled moans vibrate from my dick all the way up my spine.

"That's it Audrey, just like that." I praise her then praise her some more, which must put her body into overdrive. She grabs my dick at the base, holding it in place as she mouth fucks me.

I'm seconds away from coming, so I grab her around her head and pull her off my dick. "If I'm going to come, I'll come in that tight little pussy." I grunt out.

I'll have plenty of chances to come in her mouth, I tell myself as I miss the feel of her lips around my throbbing cock.

"Lay back kitten, I'm going to fuck that pussy now," I grunt out. Not wanting to come as soon as I sink myself deep inside of her, I calm my racing heart.

With my adjusted eyesight in the dark, I can faintly make out her figure moving to lie on the ground. "Roll that skirt up for my baby,"

Faintly hearing the ruffling of her skirt fabric, I make my way to lay on top of her. As soon as I have her face in front of mine, I lean down and take her lips into mine.

The taste of her is so sweet and addicting. Something a poor man would sell his soul to be able to have.

"I wanna feel your tight cunt choke my cock. I wanna take you bare baby," I whisper into her ear. "I'm clean, tested a few weeks ago," trying to ease her mind into me taking her raw.

"I'm clean, I have the birth control in my arm. I trust you." Her voice is hoarse and full of need.

It's all I need as I reach for my cock and slam into her full tilt. We share a moan together as it vibrates off the walls.

Her pussy is so tight and warm. I almost come at that moment.

"You ok?" I ask, running my hand along her face.

"Yes. Hayden-" she pauses. My heart tightens thinking I've hurt her in any way.

"Yea baby, what is it?" worry laced in my voice.

"I need you to fuck me, please," she asks. And I do. I give my girl just what she wants.

I start slowly, to adjust her to my size. One thrust after another, until I can't control my need for her anymore.

ONE NIGHT WITH MY NEIGHBOR

And she takes every thrust I give her. I am completely lost in her that I almost don't hear her when she asks, "harder Hayden, please fuck me harder."

What my girl wants, she gets. I hold her in place at the hips and give her every inch of my dick.

"Yes, Hayden. Oh my god," she's trying to form a coherent thought but she is lost in our moment. Just how I want her. Not thinking, but feeling how good we are together.

"Fuck Audrey! You feel so fucking good. I'm about to come, baby." I grunt out as I sink myself fully inside her over and over.

"Me too," she moans, and in the instant, both of us scream out our release.

Her moans fill my ears. The darkness of the room turns a burning white color. My orgasm shoots down my spine, through my dick, and into her tight pussy.

As I come down from my euphoric high I plant kisses all over her face. Her soft giggles fill the room. I pull out of her and without looking I run my finger along her pussy, feeling my come escaping her.

With the mixture of our two orgasms coating my finger, I bring it between us and say, "open your mouth for me baby, taste how good we are together."

Without having to see her, I know her mouth is open as I guide my finger to her mouth. I feel her tongue first then her lips wrap around my finger.

She sucks my finger clean as I pull my finger free with a popping noise escaping her mouth. I am in such awe of this woman.

I stand and adjust myself back into my pants before I lean down and help Audrey stand on her own feet. "Let's get out of here, what do you say," I throw my hand over her shoulder and guide her to the exit I looked for before we came in here.

"I don't know if my legs work," she laughs.

A.K WEAR

Without a second thought, I bend down and throw her over my shoulder as I walk toward the crisp autumn air.

SEVENTEEN
Audrey

I can't help the laugh that escapes me as Hayden slings me over his shoulder. Between the countless orgasms I've had tonight and the euphoric feeling I'm feeling right now I don't know how much I can take tonight.

My body is limp as he pushes the door, leading us into the night air. The laughter and screams of people all around us fill my ears. But the sound is muffled because all I can concentrate on is the firmness of Hayden's ass.

I want to fight him to put me down but I love the feel of him holding me in place. Placing my hands on his hips and attempting to lift my limp body, I notice the looks of the people around us.

Oh, what we must look like. I should feel ashamed. I should worry about what people will say in the coming days. The whispers, the gossip.

But all I feel is joy. Nothing can bring me down from this high that I have felt ever since laying eyes on Hayden earlier tonight.

The night's events start to flash in my memory. I honestly have had the time of my life. Hayden has given me something that no other man has been able to.

Freedom. Freedom to feel. Feel my emotions, whatever they might have been throughout the night.

Lust, anytime he's looked at me with those deep gray eyes.

Compassion for the moments that he has allowed me to cry throughout the night. Anytime Greg came into the forefront of my mind, I couldn't help but break down. Hayden was there helping me and making sure I was ok.

Even when I threw my fit in the alley about what he and I were going to be after tonight. I had no right to ask for anything more after tonight. He set the rules; a night of fun for the both of us.

And yet, he allowed me to speak out my frustrations and needs of him. He was there to listen and guide me out of my frustrations.

What more could a girl possibly ask for?

Could we be more after tonight? I know he's told me he wants more but what is more to him?

Is more; going on dates, sleeping in the same bed, seeing each other around town, and waving hello from across the street.

I know I'll take anything he is willing to give me. I am desperate for him. His kindness. His warmth. His body. Which scares me in the pit of my stomach.

The feelings that are stirring deep inside of me for this man are unlike any I have felt for any previous boyfriend.

"You can put me down now," I laugh as Hayden continues to carry me unashamed as more and more people stare at us.

"If it was up to me, I'd never put you down," he grunts out as he does in fact continue to carry me until we finally reach a sitting area.

As my feet hit the ground, I feel lightheaded. Not from being upside down for so long but by the look in Hayden's eyes as he stares at me.

The look in his eyes is all too familiar. It's the same look he's had all night. Breaking eye contact he looks around us.

Were in the back corner of the festival. The courthouse is a few yards away. It's decorated from top to bottom with fall decorations. Large orange light bulbs line the roof all the way around. The windows have wreaths on them and the steps leading to the front door have pumpkins on the sides.

This town always goes all out for their festivals. It brings the town together. Brings people from towns all around us to visit. It can be overwhelming but fun all the same.

Tonight has been unlike any time I've come for all the best reasons. The main reason is staring at me at this very moment.

I must have missed what he said when he looks at me suspiciously.

"I'm sorry, did you say something?" I laughed out loud.

"I asked if you wanted to go on a hay ride around town?" It's his turn to laugh this time. The nervousness evaporated between us.

"Sure," I answer simply. He doesn't let a second go by before he grabs my hand and starts to pull me toward the courthouse, where the line for the hay ride starts.

The line moves rather quickly since there is more than one flatbed trailer working the route.

Hayden and I wait only minutes until it was our turn to climb in. The flatbed is lined with hay bales on both sides with blankets for warmth on every other bale.

We make our way toward the center of the trailer. Hayden takes the blanket and covers our legs.

With the moon full and high in the sky, I am feeling the chill of the night for the first time. As if he senses it, Hayden takes off his leather jacket and drops it over my shoulders.

I don't pull my arms through, letting its warmth cover me. The smile of something foreign invades my senses.

The scent is familiar but I can't place it. It's mixed with the scent of him. A mixture of nature and metal.

"Thank you," I say and he doesn't say anything but just smiles that soft warm smile at me.

The hay ride takes us through town, the small shops passing us on either side. Until it turns and makes its way out of the town square.

It passes some historical markers throughout town, our ride guide giving little tidbits of historical information about little ol' Hollow Creek.

As the driver makes another turn, I realize he's driving down the street of my apartment building.

"Hey, I live on this street," Hayden says.

My eyes go wide in shock. What does he mean, he lives on this street.

Oak Street only has one set of apartments, mine. The rest of the building houses more shops, a library, and a daycare.

"Yeah, that's my apartment building right there." He points and I watch in amazement as his finger points right to the Oaks Apartment building.

"You live there?" I ask dumbfounded.

"Yeah, my best friend, you met earlier, he and I rent an apartment. We moved in a few weeks ago."

Why does he sound so nonchalant about this? Then it hits me, he doesn't know I also live there.

"That's my apartment building. I live there." I look at him and the same shock that's on my face is mirrored on his. "Apartment 4B," I add.

"Apartment 4A," he answers the question stirring in my mind.

EIGHTEEN
Hayden

She lives in my apartment building. She lives in my apartment building, on my floor. Right across the hall.

What are the fucking chances?

In this small town, the chances were pretty high now that I think about it.

But wow, my apartment building, is right across the hall. I can't help the smile that forms on my face.

Needing to hold her, I wrap my arm over her shoulder and pull her into me. "This just got interesting kitten," I kiss her temple and hold her at my side.

The chill of the night does nothing to close my rising body temperature from having her in my arms. Her warmth overtakes me as we spend the rest of the hay ride back to the town square in silence, enjoying each other and the starry night.

The people around us don't pay us any mind as they are in their conversations. Audrey and I are in our bubble of peace.

Once the car that was pulling us stops where we started, the group of us make our way off the flatbed trailer. I step down first then grab Audrey by the hips and help her down a few feet down to the ground.

I wrap my arm back around her shoulder as we make our way around the square. We've done it all tonight. Memories of our night together come flooding back.

With every passing memory, a bigger smile forms on my face and the urge to hold her tighter takes over me.

"Hayden, you're holding me tight," she gruffs out.

Realizing just how hard I'm holding her, I apologize and release her but take her hand in mine just the same.

"Wanna head home?" I ask. With the hours that have passed, the crowds have lessened.

"Yeah, I am pretty tired," she answers as I start to lead us toward the front of the festival so we can walk home.

The walk home is spent in an anticipated silence. I know we've talked about having more with each other after tonight but where does that leave us once I drop her off across the hall?

Will she want to spend the night, or invite me in? I'm itching to find out.

Before I know what she was doing, she pulls out the joints I had put in my jacket pocket. My heart races to think if she's okay with it.

The state made it legal years ago but there is still such a stigma around people who smoke pot.

"Is this... marijuana?" she asks, whispering out the word marijuana. I want to laugh out my response but I hold it back not wanting to embarrass her.

"Yeah," is all I say as we continue our walk hand in hand down the street.

"Can I try some?" she says with no emotion in her voice.

My brain misfires and the breath I inhaled gets stuck in my throat at her question.

I'm not going to tell her no but I'm just surprised that she would want to. But I guess this is her way of rebelling some more.

When she told me earlier how much of a rule follower she was for the sake of her parents, my heart ached for me. To need that kind of validation from your parents.

But mine were the complete opposite. I don't know how I would have reacted to my parents if they had taken any interest in anything I had done.

"Of course," I respond. We've stopped walking as I reach into my other jacket pocket and take out the lighter I brought as well. "Put this end in your mouth," I tell her.

She does it without thinking. "I'm going to light this end, you're going to take a small inhale, keep it in your mouth, and do not exhale until I tell you,"

She grabs the joint out of her mouth and says, "yes sir," that does something to me but I refrain from reacting.

She sets the joint back against her lips. I flick the lighter and light the end of it. I watch her take a breath, filling her mouth and lungs with the smoke.

I take the joint from her mouth, she holds the smoke in her mouth for a second, but to her, I'm sure it feels like minutes.

"Blow it out," I say and instantly she does. She coughs uncontrollably, letting the smoke take over her lungs.

I watch in real time as her eyes glaze over and she catches her breath. "That burns," she coughs out once more.

This time I didn't hold back my laugh. I don't remember the last time I laughed this hard. But it feels good.

As we make it to the front stoop of my *-our-* apartment building, she doesn't walk up the steps but sits on the middle one.

Sitting next to her, I can't help but just watch her in her high state. Her eyes are red and glazed. Her body looks less tense and free.

I hold out the weed in front of her, asking her if she wants more while not saying a word. She takes it from me, doing the same thing as before.

This time she doesn't cough as much. But she settles into the high even more.

For the next thirty minutes, she and I pass the joint back and forth until she takes the last hit. I toss the bud to the ground, grinding the reminisce into the concrete.

"Thank you for tonight," she says. "For everything. For the fun night, the stuffed cat prize, and the sex." she pauses as if she's remembering the amazing sex we've had. "Oh my god, the sex. It was wow. Amazing, wonderful. Great." She goes on and on.

I watch her in amusement, not wanting to break her train of thought, letting her finish.

"Your dick is amazing." she blurts out. And I let out the laugh that I've been holding back.

"Thank you kitten," I say low and slow.

She looks over at me. The reminisce of her high is still written all over her face. She's so cute like this.

We spend the rest of the night on the stoop in front of our apartment just talking. About anything and everything. Getting lost in each other's stories from the past and our wants for the future.

When I woke up this morning, I didn't think this was how my night would end. I hated the thought of moving to a small town. But the thought of spending my days with Audrey makes that reality that much better.

EPILOGUE: 6 MONTHS LATER
Audrey

The summer heat is piercing my skin as I walk down the street toward the town square. The large tan bolero hat shields my eyes but my exposed shoulders are radiating from the heat.

Couples holding hands walking at a leisurely pace, not knowing that I have somewhere to be. Somewhere important. Somewhere six months in the making.

The past six months have been a roller coaster with Hayden. We have been inseparable since that night at the fall festival.

My mind takes me back to that night. That night changed everything for me. It allowed me to become the person I am today.

I'm still the same person but I'm newer. Better. The old me would care what people would think of me, this new me doesn't. That's why I have the confidence that I do now.

With the help of Sami and Hayden, I have been able to find the real me hidden behind the people pleaser.

Sami and I hang around the tattoo shop most nights. When we're not at the bookstore and bakery we ended up opening up a few doors down. Marcus and her are always at each other's throats nowadays. The tension is there, Hayden and I both see it. I've been begging her to just tell Marcus that she has feelings for him.

Like me, Sami has been hurt in the past. She keeps her heart guarded. Marcus is going to have his hands full if he ever takes the plunge and tells her.

The old me would never have worn what I'm wearing right now. The daisy duke ripped denim shorts, cover just enough of my ass. My pink crop top with a band that Hayden loves.

I am a new person, and I love myself that much more. Hayden is to blame or to thank.

As I make my way closer to the tattoo shop, my palms start to sweat. Not from the summer heat, but by the nervousness with what Hayden and I had planned that night six months ago.

It's the day Hayden takes my tattoo virginity.

He opened up his tattoo shop a few weeks after the fall festival. Some people around town didn't like it but for the most part, they have been very successful.

He and Marcus were able to hire four more artists to fill the open stations. His schedule is booked out for the next six months.

There are nights when we are together that all he does is draw. It doesn't bother me. It's him doing what makes him happy. What he enjoys and I won't be the girlfriend to ever make him feel bad about it.

Just being in the same room as him makes me happy. I'm content.

The bell above the door rings out as I make my way into the shop. Stephanie, the receptionist, smiles at me. She's also become a good friend of mine.

I wasn't someone that had a lot of friends. That was mostly Greg's doing. He didn't want me going out or making friends. He wanted me at home, waiting for him to get home at all hours of the day.

But now, I have friends, a social life, and honestly, I'm just thriving.

"Hi Steph," I smile at her as she types on the tablet on top of her counter.

"Hey girl, I've checked you in, you can head back there, he's been waiting for you all morning." Her knowing smile lands as intended.

I have been waiting for this moment for longer. A nervousness courses through me as I walk down the aisle.

Jett, one of the new hires standing over a man as he tattoos his exposed back. Grunts of pain come from the man. Jett sees me walk by, he rolls his eyes and smiles at me. I smile back and make my way further down the aisle.

All but one station is being used as the artists tattoo their clients. The buzzing sounds of the tattoo guns reverberating off the walls.

I make it to the last station where Hayden is. He's hunched over his table as he's playing with his inks and supplies.

"Hey handsome," I say, my tone laced with a sexiness reserved only for Hayden.

He jumps in surprise. Realizing it's me, his eyes run down my body. I love it when he looks at me like this like he could eat me alive. Not for the lack of trying.

I can feel him everywhere.

His eyes finally land on my eyes and pierce me with the same feeling I have felt for the past six months.

Lust.

Fighting the feeling of wanting him to take me here and now, I step into his station, and without saying a word I lean on my tip toes and kiss his cheek.

"How do you want me?" I ask playfully as I make my way to his tattoo chair that he's flatted for me to be able to lie down.

"Anyway I can have you, baby," he grunts and winks at me.

Removing my hat, I set it in the extra chair in the corner with my crossbody bag next to it. I grab my shirt at the hem of my shirt, raise it above my head, and toss it at Hayden's head.

The look of shock and sexual frustration is hard to miss on his face. I can't help but laugh.

"Audrey, what the fuck," he grunts out throwing my shirt back at me.

I laugh as I catch it and say, "I didn't want anything getting in the way." I wink playfully.

He laughs but I can see he's fighting his anger. He turns around back to his desk as he gets the rest of the supplies ready.

I can hear him put a pair of black latex gloves on. He pours black and white ink into small tubs and then turns his tattoo gun on. The buzz hits my ears and my whole body vibrates in anticipation.

As he sits in his small chair he rolls over to me as I'm lying flat in the tattoo chair.

"Ready?" he asks. I nod nervously at him.

The first sting of pain courses through my body. The pain is aching in my chest. "Ouch," I scream in a muffled yell as my hand covers my mouth.

"I'll make it quick kitten, hang on tight."

The next thirty minutes go by at an agonizingly slow pace. Seconds turn into minutes, minutes into hours. I feel as though I have been here for days when I hear him finally say, "all done, don't move,"

Sweat has built up on my forehead as I lay there zoning in on the ceiling tiles. That was the worst pain I have ever felt in my life. "I am never doing that again," I huff out.

Hayden laughs at me as he sprays a paper towel with a solution and wipes it gently over the area on my hip. "Go take a look," he says.

I stand and walk over to the floor mirror in the corner of his area. A smile lifts as I look at the black outline of a cat on my hip. It's simple line work, but it's perfect.

A reminder of that night when I asked him if he would ever tattoo me. The night after, I went over to his apartment and asked if he really would. He said yes but he told me to take some time to think about it. So here we are, six months of nagging and waiting.

"I love it," I turn and face Hayden who is rolling up the table cover and all the supplies together and throwing it in the trash can. He smiles at me with pride.

"Come here, I need to wrap it." I walk over to him, watching as he kneels next to me. He takes a clear plastic out of its wrapping and covers the tattoo.

He explains to me how to take care of it, but I'm not listening. I'm lost at this moment. What this moment means.

It's another moment that changes me. Change us. This is more than a tattoo. This is a moment that brings Hayden and me closer together.

"Hayden," I moan.

He stands, kisses my forehead, and starts to turn, "yea baby," he answers.

"Take me home, please," I beg, knowing that he loves it when I do. He's taken me every time I've asked. This moment won't be any different.

He sees the lust in my eyes as he walks over to me and kisses me. For the past six months, his lips have been my favorite place to be.

I feel safe and taken care of every time his lips are on me, anywhere.

"I'll meet you at home, I have to calm my dick before walking out there," he whispers as he leans into my ear. "But when I get home, I want you naked and ready for me." he bites down on my earlobe right before he pulls away.

I am in a constant state of need when I am around Hayden. I rush to put my shirt on. I grab my bag and hat and practically run out of the tattoo shop.

Sprinting home, some people I pass give me judgmental looks. And in this moment I don't give a fuck what they think.

The End

MORE BOOKS

Bloodline of New York Series
Mine to Keep a dark mafia stalker
Mine to Have a dark mafia marriage of convenience
Book 3 coming in 2024
Book 4 coming in 2024
One Night Series
One Night Book 2 coming in 2024

About the Author

AK Wear is a Bosnian American living the dream. She lives in Texas with my husband and daughter. She is a lover of all things romance. Her love of reading started while she was learning the English language. But it wasn't until later in life that she found a love for writing. Like most, she found the book community in 2020 while being stuck at home during the shutdown. Through her love of reading, she is now living her dream of writing the stories of her heart.
Stay in touch through Facebook, Instagram and Tiktok

Made in the USA
Columbia, SC
15 February 2024